SEP. 1 8 2021

NO LONGER PROPERTY OF
SEATTLE PUBLIC LIBRARY

A JIGSAW JONES MYSTERY

The Case of the
Bear Scare

D1021094

Read more Jigsaw Jones Mysteries by James Preller

A JIGSAW JONES MYSTERY

The Case of the Bear Scare

by James Preller

illustrated by Jamie Smith

cover illustration by R. W. Alley

FEIWEL AND FRIENDS

New York

A Feiwel and Friends Book
An imprint of Macmillan Publishing Group, LLC
120 Broadway, New York, NY 10271

Jigsaw Jones: The Case of the Bear Scare.
Copyright © 2002 by James Preller. All rights reserved.
Printed in the United States of America by LSC Communications,
Harrisonburg, Virginia.

Our books may be purchased in bulk for promotional, educational, or business
use. Please contact your local bookseller or the Macmillan Corporate and
Premium Sales Department at (800) 221-7945 ext. 5442 or by email at
MacmillanSpecialMarkets@macmillan.com.

Library of Congress Cataloging-in-Publication Data is available.

ISBN 978-1-250-20754-8 (paperback) / ISBN 978-1-250-20755-5 (ebook)

Book design by Véronique Lefèvre Sweet

Illustrations by Jamie Smith

Feiwel and Friends logo designed by Filomena Tuosto

First Feiwel and Friends edition, 2019
Originally published by Scholastic in 2002
Art used with permission from Scholastic

1 3 5 7 9 10 8 6 4 2

mackids.com

In memory of Steve Irwin, "The Crocodile Hunter,"
who inspired the character Lightning Lou

CONTENTS

Lightning Lou

The moment I walked into my classroom, Stringbean Noonan grabbed my shirt with both fists and exclaimed, "Did you hear, Jigsaw? DID YOU HEAR?!"

"How could I *not* hear?" I snapped back. "You're screaming in my face."

"Whoops, sorry. I'm just excited because Lightning Lou is coming today!" Stringbean exclaimed. "He's going to talk to the whole school!"

"Lightning . . . who?" I wondered.

"Lou," Stringbean answered.

"Ah, Lou."

"Bless you," Stringbean replied.

"Huh?"

"You just sneezed," he claimed. "You said, '*Ah-choo*.'"

"Did not," I said.

"Did too," Stringbean countered.

"Stringbean. Trust me," I said. "I didn't sneeze."

Stringbean pulled on his earlobe. "Then why did you say, '*Ah-choo*'?"

"I said, 'Ah, Lou,'" I replied. "Get it? *Ah, Lou*. It's like, a-ha, but it's *Lou* instead of *ha*."

Stringbean shook his head sadly. "You're a strange dude, Jigsaw."

"*I'm* strange?!" I protested.

Stringbean smiled kindly. "It's okay, Jigsaw. I still like you."

I asked. "Who's Lightning Lou, anyway?"

Stringbean stared at me in shock. "He's the animal guy on television. *The Lightning Lou Animal Review*!"

"Oh, the Australian guy!" I said, remembering the weekly television show. "Didn't he once get trampled by a wombat or something?"

"A wildebeest," Stringbean corrected. "Yeah, but he's here today—at school! How cool is that?"

"So cool we'll need hats and mittens," I answered.

Just then, Mila Yeh and Geetha Nair walked into the room. "Did you hear?" Stringbean

howled. "DID YOU HEAR?! Lightning Lou is coming to our school!"

"Lightning . . . who?" Geetha asked.

I didn't stick around for the rest. I'd seen that movie before. I went to my seat instead. Our classroom, room 201, was set up with big tables. Actually, each table was just four desks shoved together. The other kids at my table were Athena Lorenzo, Joey Pignattano, and Helen Zuckerman.

We were lucky. Our teacher, Ms. Gleason, was probably the nicest person in the world—if you didn't count the Tooth Fairy.

And I didn't.

We liked her and she liked us right back. She even liked Bobby Solofsky, which proves that Ms. Gleason was an especially kind and patient person. Because liking Bobby Solofsky wasn't easy. I figured it was easier to like kale. But my Grams says I've got to try to see the good in everybody. So I try. Only with Solofsky, I have to try extra, *extra* hard.

Keen as Mustard

Maybe I should explain something. I run a detective agency with my partner, Mila Yeh. She's been my friend since forever. We've solved all sorts of mysteries together, from buried treasure to stolen bicycles. We get a dollar a day for our troubles. Don't tell anyone, but we'd do it for nothing.

Probably.

I was doodling, dreaming of baseball, when a voice called to me from far away.

"Earth to Jigsaw. Earth to Jigsaw. Come in, Jigsaw."

I felt a tap on my shoulder.

"Huh?"

I looked around the room. Everyone was staring at me. Ms. Gleason stood next to me, smiling.

"He's daydreaming again!" Ralphie Jordan announced.

I bolted upright in my chair.

"I realize today is Friday," Ms. Gleason said sweetly. "It has been a long week for everyone. Please try to pay attention, Jigsaw."

I nodded, embarrassed.

"As I was saying," Ms. Gleason told the class, "Lightning Lou is from Australia. Can anyone tell me what language they speak in Australia?"

"That's easy," Joey Pignattano said. "Australian!"

"Not exactly, Joey," Ms. Gleason replied. "They speak English. But if you have seen

Lightning Lou on television, you know he uses a lot of Australian slang."

"What's slang?" Helen asked.

"Hmmm, how can I explain this?" wondered Ms. Gleason aloud. "There's standard English. Those are the words we find in most dictionaries. Slang is a group of made-up words and phrases."

Ms. Gleason sighed when she saw our blank faces.

"For example, someone from Australia might say 'G'day' instead of 'Hello.'"

Stringbean Noonan's hand shot to the ceiling. He gushed, "In Australian slang, they call parents 'oldies.' And they call little kids 'ankle-biters'!"

Everybody thought that was funny.

"A friend is called 'mate,'" Danika Starling told us.

Eddie Becker said, "I love it when

Lightning Lou gets mad. He always says, 'Crikey! Wouldn't it rot your socks!'"

Ms. Gleason said, "Instead of our weekly spelling words, I've put together a list of Australian slang words. I'll hand it out later. I think you will like learning Australian slang as much as I did."

Ms. Gleason looked at the wall clock. "Okay, boys and girls. It's time to get to the gym to meet Lightning Lou." She winked at us and added, "Personally, I'm *keen as mustard* to hear him speak!"

Chapter 3

Crikey!

The gym smelled like sweaty socks. I sat next to Mila on the hard wooden floor. More and more kids crowded into the room. We squished together in tight rows, like too many crayons in a box. Our principal, Mr. Rogers, waved his arms like a traffic cop.

Suddenly, the lights flickered.

"*Crikey!*" a voice bellowed through a microphone.

Heads turned in every direction. A hand pointed. Excited shouts went out. "There he is! In the back of the room! Look, it's Lightning Lou!"

I recognized him instantly. He was dressed in brown safari shorts, a tan short-sleeve shirt, and a floppy brown jungle hat. And, oh yeah, he had a huge snake draped around his shoulders.

Other than that, he fit right in.

Lightning Lou shouted, *"G'day, mates!"* He strode to the front of the room, ready for adventure. Lightning Lou was short and stocky. He smiled at the audience, white teeth twinkling. He wore a cast on his right arm. I guess Stringbean was right. Lightning Lou really did get trampled by a wilde-beest.

"Am I ever *knackered*," Lightning Lou screamed at us. "I just flew in from *Oz*. Boy, are my arms tired!"

He laughed at his own joke.

"*Knackered* means tired," Mila whispered

into my ear. "And *Oz* is another word for Australia."

"How do you know?" I asked.

"I just do," Mila answered.

Lightning Lou spent the next half hour showing us slides of animals he'd met in his

travels. All the while he talked in that funny
way of his. He shouted "*Crikey!*" every few
minutes. Or said things like, "I'm as proud
as a rat with a gold tooth!"

It was pretty confusing.

After a while, Lightning Lou told us that

he enjoyed our little chin-wag. "In a few ticks I'll have to shove off," he said. "But I'll answer a few questions before I leave."

Ralphie Jordan stood up. "What are you doing here?" he asked. "Aren't you supposed to be on television or something?"

Lightning Lou laughed. "I came here to do some research on black bears," he answered. "We'll probably film a show."

"Black bears!" Bobby Solofsky scoffed. "There are no bears around here!"

Lightning Lou smiled. "Sure there are, mate," he replied. "And I aim to find me one."

Bears

Kim Lewis raised her hand. "My father read a story in the newspaper about a bear who walked right into somebody's backyard."

Lightning Lou nodded. "That's right. It happens every spring."

"Why don't bears just stay in the woods?" Kim asked.

"Bears are territorial," Lou explained. "That means each male bear stakes out an area and calls it home. If there's a big male around, then a smaller male will leave to find his own place to live.

"Bears mostly rest during the day," he continued, "but they can travel a long way at night. A young male will often follow a river until he finds a place he likes. He'll eat plants and small animals as he goes."

"We have a big river close by," Nicole Rodriguez murmured.

"Yes, you do," Lightning Lou said. "And black bears are excellent swimmers. They'll even swim across a river if they like the smell of something."

Lightning Lou glanced at his watch. "Okay, mates. Time for one more question. Then I have to untie the frog."

"Untie the frog?" I asked Mila.

"It means he has to leave," Mila whispered.

Australian slang. Yeesh. I give up.

Bigs Maloney raised his hand. "Mr. Lou, sir? I mean, Mr. Lightning. Er, um, Mr. Whatever-You-Call-Yourself. I have a question. How would you know if a bear was hanging around your backyard?"

"Great question," Lightning Lou said. "Most of the time, bears pass through without anybody ever knowing it. But sometimes they leave clues. Like muddy tracks. Or they'll nuzzle around in a compost heap. Bears like melon rinds, for example. And bears *love* birdseed and berries. They're very curious, too. A black bear might even go up to a house and look through the window."

Our principal, Mr. Rogers, seemed a little uneasy. "If one of our students ever saw a bear," he announced, "he or she should stay inside and call the police. Isn't that right, Lightning Lou?"

Lightning Lou frowned a bit, tilting his head back and forth. "Yes, you should stay inside," he admitted. "But to be honest with you, I worry more about the safety of the bear than the people. You see, black bears don't want to hurt anyone. Yes, they can be dangerous. And a female *will* protect her

cubs. But bears have terrific manners. They will leave you alone if you leave them alone."

"What would the police do?" Ralphie Jordan asked. "They can't take a bear away in handcuffs!"

Lightning Lou shook his head and sighed heavily. "Sadly, bears that wander into crowded areas are often destroyed. After all, bears are wild, large, and very powerful. The best thing to do if you see a bear is to stay away from it. Contact animal control

experts. They'll put the bear to sleep with a small dart. Then they'll return the bear deep into the woods. This way, no one gets hurt—including the poor bear, who is only looking for a home.

"And now," he announced, "I must really be going. I'll be staying at the Holiday Hotel for a few days. Maybe I'll see you around town. And remember this . . ."

Lightning Lou threw his hat into the audience. He put his hands to his mouth and hollered, "*Crikey!*"

A hundred voices answered with a great shout: "CRIIIKEEEY!"

I didn't say a word. I just stared at the hat that had fallen into my lap.

Chapter 5

Pancakes

"Jigsaw, take off that hat at the breakfast table," my mother ordered.

"This is Lightning Lou's hat," I protested.

"Not at the table," my mother insisted.

Oldies. Crikey. They have this thing about hats and tables that I will never understand. What's the big deal? Besides, I wasn't keen as mustard to eat breakfast in the first place.

Grams says I'm a fussy eater. My mom says I'm just impossible. But my dad never complains. He just says, "I was the same way when I was growing up."

"You're not helping," my mother complained.

"It's the truth," my dad replied. "When I was a kid, I wouldn't have eaten a blueberry pancake if you paid me."

I nodded in agreement. That's what I liked about my dad. He was once a boy himself. He understands.

"Theodore," my mother said. (She only calls me Theodore when she's unhappy.) "Grams made these delicious pancakes as a special treat. You should at least *try* one. You might like it."

"But I don't like blueberry pancakes," I said.

"Why not?"

"They have blueberries in them," I reasoned.

"Duh," my sister Hillary commented. "That's why they call them *blueberry pancakes*, Einstein."

I gave her the evil eye. Hillary smirked, "Don't stare at me, zombie face."

"I picked these blueberries fresh last season," Grams said. She flipped another pancake. "I froze them so we could enjoy blueberries all year long. They are delicious, Jigsaw!" She popped one into her mouth and made a big show out of how wonderful it tasted.

I wasn't buying it.

"Take a bite," my mom insisted.

I clamped my mouth shut.

"Or no puzzles for a week."

So that's how it was going to be. I decided to bargain.

"Just one bite?" I asked.

"Yes, one bite," she answered.

I slowly lifted the fork toward my mouth. But for some reason, my mouth wouldn't open.

"Eat it, Jigsaw," Hillary said.

"I'm trying," I mumbled through locked lips. I wanted to tell my mom how sometimes a mouth does whatever it wants. But I couldn't because my mouth didn't want to talk about it.

"Hey, Jigsaw! There's one of your friends at the door," my oldest brother, Billy, called from the next room. "It's a girl!"

"A girl?" I said, dropping my fork.

"She says it's an emergency," Billy replied.

I excused myself from the table. I found Lucy Hiller waiting on our front stoop. Her arms were crossed, her toes were tapping, and it looked like she'd seen a ghost.

Chapter 6

Home Alone

"Jigsaw, thank goodness you're home. I have a mystery for you," Lucy began.

"Okay," I said. "For a dollar a day, I make problems go away. What's up?"

Lucy shook her head. "I can't explain it. I need you to come to my house. There's something I need to show you."

"I'll call Mila," I replied. "We'll get there as soon as we can."

"You know where I live, right?" Lucy asked.

"Sure, I've been by there before. It's the big red house on Merkle Stream Drive. You have a little patch of woods in your backyard."

"That the place," Lucy answered. "But hurry, okay? I'm scared out of my mind to be home alone."

An hour later, Mila and I parked our bikes in front of Lucy's house. The front door opened a crack. A blue eyeball peered through the opening. "Quick. Come in," Lucy urged. She

opened the door with a sudden *whoosh.* We stepped inside. Lucy leaned against the door and slammed it shut.

Lucy's eyes were nothing special. She had two of them, one on each side of her face. But her hair was a whirl of curls. She wore a huge flower-print T-shirt, bright blue leggings, a pink plastic belt, and a pair of red go-go boots. Rainbows were probably jealous of Lucy's closet.

Lucy led us into her living room. Mila sat on the couch next to me. Lucy plopped down, cross-legged, on the floor. The television flickered and buzzed. Lucy reached for the remote and hit the MUTE button. I flipped open my detective journal and waited.

Lucy twirled a finger through her hair. She chewed her lip.

"You seem nervous," Mila observed.

Lucy nodded. She took a deep breath, then smiled for the first time. "I'm really

glad you guys came. I've been afraid to be home alone since it happened."

"Great movie," I commented.

"Huh?"

"*Home Alone*," I said. "It's a classic. An oldie but a goodie."

Mila rolled her eyes. "Where's your family?" she asked Lucy.

Lucy shrugged. "My parents had to go to a wedding. My brother, Alex, is *supposed* to be watching me. But he's playing basketball at Duffy Dyer's house."

"So it's just us," I said.

"Yeah, just us," Lucy repeated. "And whoever—or *what*ever—is out there." Lucy pointed past the window into the woods beyond her backyard.

"What are you talking about?" I asked. "Did you see something out there? Was it a robber?"

"Worse," Lucy answered.

"An animal?" Mila guessed. "Like a stray dog or something?"

"Worse than a stray dog," Lucy repeated.

"Did you see Bigfoot tiptoe through the tulips?" I joked.

Lucy looked to the carpet. Her face went pale.

"A *bear* . . . ?" Mila guessed.

Lucy slapped a few dollars into Mila's hand. "*You're* the detectives. What are you waiting for? Start detectin'!"

Chapter 7

Growl

We stepped into Lucy's large, sprawling backyard. Tall trees towered above us. The sky was clear and bright. A light breeze blew, carrying with it all the promises of spring.

"Look at this, Jigsaw." Mila held up a wooden pole that had been snapped in half. At the top, there was a bird feeder.

"It would take a very chubby squirrel to do that," I quipped.

"Or a bear," Mila stated. "They love birdseed, remember? Lightning Lou told us that."

I remembered.

We searched the yard for bear tracks but didn't find any. "It hasn't rained in a while," Mila pointed out. "The ground is hard and firm. A bear might not have left tracks."

Mila was right, as usual. In the far corner of Lucy's backyard, I noticed a compost pile ringed with wire fencing. Beyond it lay the woods. The compost looked like last week's garbage to me. Banana peels, coffee grounds, melon rinds, and other scraps.

"What a smelly mess," I groaned.

Mila tapped her front tooth thoughtfully. "I still don't see paw prints. No scratch marks on the trees. It's hard to tell for sure."

Growl.

"Shhh," Mila whispered. She grabbed my arm and squeezed. "Did you hear that?"

I listened.

Growl, rumble, gurgle, growl.

She squeezed tighter.

"What's that growling sound?!" Mila asked, her eyes wide with fear.

GROWL.

Mila backed up a step. Then another.

I smiled. "Relax, partner," I said. "That's my stomach. I didn't eat breakfast this morning."

"Jigsaw!" snapped Mila. "Tell your stomach to pipe down! You nearly scared me to death." She turned and stomped back into the house.

Lucy was waiting for us in the kitchen. "What do you guys think?"

I opened my detective journal and wrote:

CLIENT: Lucy Hiller
CASE: The Bear Scare

I jotted down a few notes. "You didn't see anything?" I asked Lucy.

She shook her head.

"Did you hear anything?" Mila asked.

Lucy lifted her shoulders and let them drop. "I don't know. Maybe some noises. I didn't pay much attention to them."

"What kind of noises?" Mila asked.

Lucy thought for a moment. "Rustling noises," she concluded.

"Like leaves?"

"Not exactly," Lucy answered. "It was more like a stomping-through-the-bushes kind of sound."

"When?" I asked.

"Right before I called," Lucy said. "I looked out the back window. I like watching the birds when I eat my Eggos. That's when I noticed the bird feeder had been knocked down."

Mila pointed out the window. "Those woods. How far back do they go?"

"Not too far," Lucy said. "There's Merkle's Stream, then a big hill. There are more houses on the other side of the hill."

Mila murmured, "Hmmmm."

"What do you mean, 'hmmmm'?" I asked.

Mila sat down heavily. "Merkle's Stream goes for a few miles. It flows from the river."

The words of Lightning Lou echoed in my ears. He had said, *A young male will often follow a river.* And if a bear will follow a river, a bear might also follow a stream. It all made sense.

"May I use your phone?" I asked Lucy.

"It depends," she said, eyes narrowing. "Who are you going to call?"

"Nine-one-one," I said. "This case is too big for us. We should notify the police."

"No way," Lucy said. She crossed her arms and glared at me.

"Take it easy, Lucy. I'm just trying to help," I countered.

"No police," Lucy demanded. "If there's a bear out there, I don't want anything to happen to him. You heard Lightning Lou. Sometimes innocent bears get hurt."

"But, Lucy, it may be a *real bear*!" I argued. "With *real teeth* and *real claws*. We're not talking about Winnie-the-Pooh."

"It's not his fault he's a bear," Lucy snapped back. "Let's leave him alone. Just pretend we never saw anything. And, well, we didn't. Did we?"

Lucy crossed her arms. Slowly, the expression on her face softened. "Look, it might not even *be* a bear. You said so yourself. We'd all feel pretty silly if the police came and it turned out to be an angry woodchuck."

"Lucy has a point," Mila noted.

I sighed. "This feels like a mistake to me."

"No police," Lucy repeated. "At least not until we have proof. Is it a deal?"

"Okay," I agreed.

"Let's go, Mila. We've got somewhere to be."

"Where are we going?" Mila asked.

"To the library," I replied. "Then back to my tree house. I'll feel safer there—it's ten feet above the ground."

Chapter 8

In the Tree House

Stringbean Noonan and Joey Pignattano joined us. We needed all the help we could get. Stringbean already knew a lot about bears. He watched nature shows all the time. And Joey, well, he was a nice guy to have around.

Mila spread the books on the tree house floor. "Here are all the books about bears that we could find," she said. "We need to learn as much about them as possible."

We each picked a book and started reading. Every few minutes, somebody would share an interesting fact. Stringbean said, "There are three species of bears in North America: brown, black, and polar. A grizzly bear is a brown bear," he explained. "They mostly live out West."

Mila added, "And polar bears live in one of the coldest spots on earth—the Arctic Circle."

"Don't forget Teddy bears!" Joey said.

"Say what?" I asked.

"It says here they got their name from President Theodore Roosevelt," Joey explained. "Write it down, Jigsaw. It may be an important clue!"

"Seriously?" I asked.

Joey was as serious as a math quiz. I wrote down Teddy bear to keep him happy.

"You never know," Joey said.

"Some people never do," I murmured. I returned to hunting down bear facts in the book on my lap.

I held up my book. "Anybody want to see a picture of bear poop?"

"Gross, Jigsaw," Mila exclaimed.

"It's research," I replied. "It's important to know what this stuff looks like."

Stringbean and Joey peered over my shoulder. "They call it *scat*," I explained. "I guess that beats calling it 'poop' all the time. Sounds more professional."

"Too bad we didn't find any at Lucy's house," Mila mused. "That would have been all the proof we needed."

Stringbean nodded thoughtfully.

Suddenly, my dog, Rags, barked below. Joey stopped talking and looked down. His face went white.

Mila noticed Joey's nervousness and teased him with a song:

> *"The bear climbed up in the tree house.*
> *The bear climbed up in the tree house.*
> *The bear climbed up in the tree house . . .*
> *To eat Joey and me!"*

"Better change your tune," I suggested to Mila. "That song's getting on Joey's nerves. Besides, bears can't climb trees."

Stringbean clucked with his tongue. "*Grizzly bears* can't climb trees," he said. "But black bears can. They do it all the time."

"Why didn't you tell us sooner?!" I exclaimed.

"I didn't think of it sooner," Stringbean said.

"That's just great," I muttered. "Here we are, up in a tree. And down there somewhere is a hungry bear who happens to like climbing trees. Let's get inside, and fast."

Chapter 9

A Tricky Code

I dug out my homework folder. I thought it might be fun to look at the slang words Ms. Gleason had given us.

It read:

AUSTRALIAN SLANG WORDS

BINGLE	An accident	LUGS	Ears
BITIES	Insects	MATE	Friend
BUSH TELLY	Campfire	MATILDA	Sleeping bag
DOG AND BONE	Telephone	OLDIES	Parents
JABBER	Talk	OZ	Australia
JOE BLAKE	Snake	YABBER	Talk a lot

A knock sounded at my door. "Jigsaw, telephone!"

Dog and bone, I thought. Rhyming slang.

It was Stringbean Noonan. "Hi, Jigsaw."

"G'day, mate," I answered. I was beginning to get the hang of this Australian slang.

"Er, yeah," Stringbean replied. "I was thinking about the bear. What if you called Lightning Lou?"

"I don't think that's such a good idea," I answered. "A hotshot TV star doesn't want to mess around with kids like us."

"No, no, he does!" Stringbean protested. "He said so himself. Remember?! He's doing research on bears. He wants to do a television show about bears. Lightning Lou would *love* to find out about this."

"Well, maybe you're right," I said. "Just the same, I'd like to get proof that there really was a bear in Lucy's backyard."

"Bear scat would do it," Stringbean said.

"Yeah," I murmured. "The real poop."

"And if you found bear droppings, then would you call Lightning Lou?" Stringbean asked.

"In a heartbeat," I answered.

There was a long silence on the other end of the phone. "Um, Jigsaw . . ."

"Yes, Stringbean?"

"Can I come? I mean, if you do call Lightning Lou. It would be great to meet him again. He's sort of my hero."

"Sure, Stringbean," I answered. "You'll be the first to know."

"Lightning Lou told us he was staying at the Holiday Hotel," Stringbean said. "I even looked up the phone number for you."

I wrote down the number and said bye. It was a good thing, too. Because my *lugs* hurt from all that *yabbering*.

I took out my detective journal. It helped me to review the facts of the case. I got inspired and drew a picture of a bear, growling and snarling. Hopefully I'd never meet him in real life.

Before bed, I wrote a message to Mila. We send all our messages in code. I used a

Vowel Code. See, the five vowels are A, E, I, O, and U. When you use a Vowel Code, you switch the vowels a little. The vowel A in the real word becomes E in the code word, E becomes I, I becomes O, O becomes U, and U becomes A.

My message was simple:

O YEBBIRID WOTH STRONGBIEN
UN THI DUG END BUNI.

It really said:

I YABBERED WITH STRINGBEAN
ON THE DOG AND BONE.

Cool, huh?

Scat!

Mila and I went back to Lucy's house bright and early Sunday morning. We found Stringbean Noonan waiting for us on Lucy Hiller's front steps. Lucy sat beside him.

"I thought you might need some help," Stringbean offered.

"Thanks," I replied. "Okay, let's spread out. And watch where you step."

"What are we looking for?" Lucy asked.

"Winnie-the-Poop," I joked.

Lucy made a face. "On second thought, I'll wait inside."

A few minutes later, Stringbean cried out, "Found one!"

We gathered around. There we were, the three of us, staring at a pile of bear poop. Funny thing was, it didn't seem gross or anything. It was sort of, um, muddy and leafy, with lots of blueberries mashed up in it. Still, I felt a chill run through me. A real, living bear had been right here where I was standing. Strong and wild and very dangerous.

Mila spoke first. "Here's the proof," she said. "Now let's get inside."

"And call Lightning Lou," Stringbean said. "Right, Jigsaw? Maybe he'll bring a cameraman. We might even get on TV!"

Stringbean didn't seem the least bit worried about becoming some bear's idea of a nice breakfast. He was happy and excited. As if finding bear scat made it the greatest day on earth. Strange kid, that Stringbean Noonan. He was afraid of his own shadow.

He was afraid of lightning, dentists, and bees. But not bears. Go figure.

Lightning Lou was thrilled by my phone call. "By crikey!" he exclaimed. "A bear! The fair dinkum? Really? I'll rock on over." He hung up before I could say much else.

"What did he say? What did he say?" Stringbean asked, tugging on my sleeve.

I scratched my head. "He said, er, 'I'll rock on over.'"

Mila nodded. "He'll be here in a minute."

Crikey.

Just as Stringbean had hoped, Lightning Lou arrived with a cameraman. Except it was a camera*woman*. She said her name was Dee-Dee, and she was nice-nice.

Mr. and Mrs. Hiller stood outside on their deck, scratching their heads. They blinked a lot and slurped coffee. "A bear? Here?" Mrs. Hiller kept repeating.

Mr. Hiller frowned. "Let's wait inside, shall we?"

Meanwhile, Lightning Lou glanced around the yard. Stringbean stayed by his side like a faithful puppy. The rest of us tagged along—me, Mila, and Lucy, who seemed to feel braver with Lightning Lou on the scene.

"Those woods?" he asked.

"They lead to a stream," I said.

"And the stream leads to a river," Mila added.

Lou nodded.

I showed him the smashed bird feeder.

He glanced at it, then looked away. "Where's the scat at, mate?"

I showed him.

Lightning Lou knelt down on his hands

and knees. "The size is right. But something seems dodgy about this." He fixed me with a gaze. "Is this some kind of shonky business?"

"Dodgy? Shonky?" I asked. "*Huh*?"

Lightning Lou brought his nose close to the bear scat. He smelled deeply, frowning all the while. Then he stuck his thumb into the middle of it, just like Little Jack Horner. Grossed me out the door.

Lou stood up, shaking his head. "Very shonky indeed," he said. "Sorry, Jigsaw, Mila, Lucy, Stringbean. But you've been tricked."

"Tricked?" I asked.

"Yup," Lightning Lou replied. "Come on, Dee-Dee. Let's get something to eat. I'm hungrier than a koala in a gum tree."

He eyed me closely. "You're a detective, right?" he asked.

I nodded.

"You are missing an important clue, mate,"

he said. Then Lightning Lou did a curious thing. He rubbed his belly and said, "I'd love a blueberry muffin right about now. Too bad blueberries aren't in season."

He gave me a long, slow wink. Then he

walked away.

"Lightning Lou?" Stringbean called out. "Where are you going?!"

There was no answer. Lightning Lou just

kept on walking. Down the path. Into his van. And out of our lives.

Stringbean called out one last time, "Don't you want to put me on TV?!"

That's when I knew.

Chapter
11

Putting the Pieces Together

"Sorry, Lucy. We didn't do our best work on this case," I grumbled. "Isn't that right, Stringbean?"

He coughed. "Excuse me?"

"Let's take a little walk," I said.

It was like a small parade. I marched into Lucy's backyard, with Mila and Lucy following. Stringbean dragged behind.

I picked up the broken bird feeder and ran my thumb across the broken edge. "Look." I showed Mila. "Here's a clue we missed."

I gave Mila the magnifying glass. "Half of the pole is perfectly flat, and the rest is splintered off," she observed. "Like it was cut halfway through with a saw."

I took what was left of the pole and handed it to Stringbean. "Go ahead. Try to break it."

Stringbean tried and frowned. He handed the pole back to me.

I gave it a try. Nothing doing. "This pole is pretty thick," I explained. "A bear could break it. But a skinny kid? No way. He'd need to cut it halfway through first. Then he could break it."

Lucy glanced at Stringbean.

Stringbean became very interested in the tops of his sneakers. He stared down in silence.

"The next clue was even easier," I said. "But we missed that one, too." I led them back to the pile of bear scat. Or whatever it was.

"Blueberries," I said. "That makes sense, right? Bears love blueberries. Everybody knows that, right, Stringbean? Except there's

one problem. Lightning Lou figured it out instantly. My Grams would have known it, too. Fortunately, Lightning Lou was nice enough to give me a little hint before he left. He said he wanted blueberry muffins, but blueberries aren't in season."

Mila snapped her fingers. "Blueberries aren't ripe until late summer! There are no blueberries around here right now!"

I nodded. "Isn't that right, Stringbean?"

He shrugged.

I reached down and picked up the bear scat.

Lucy gasped. "YUCK!"

"It's not real poop," I explained. "So how did you do it, Stringbean? Did you wake up early this morning and throw a bunch of leaves and junk into a blender? Did you add a scoop of blueberries?"

Stringbean looked upset. He nodded once. Yes.

"It's okay, Stringbean," I said. "I think I know why you did it. You wanted to be on TV. You wanted to be friends with Lightning Lou. It was that simple.

"When he came to town, you saw your chance. So you created this whole phony bear scare. That's why you weren't afraid up in the tree house. You knew there weren't any bears around."

"You're right, Jigsaw," Stringbean admitted. "I confess—take me to jail."

I laughed. "No one is going to jail, Stringbean. In fact, that was pretty smart thinking. You almost pulled it off." I looked around Lucy's backyard. "You picked the perfect place, too. The woods, the stream. It all made sense. I'm impressed."

Stringbean looked surprised. "You are?"

I smiled at him. "Sure I am, mate."

Mila pulled from her pocket the money Lucy had given us.

"You're giving it back?" Lucy said in surprise.

"Well, sort of," Mila answered. "I think Stringbean is the one who should pay."

"Agreed?" I asked him.

Stringbean nodded. In fact, he looked relieved.

And that was that.

We'd solved another case. Call it *The Bear Scare That Wasn't*. Only this time, we could not have done it without the help of Lightning Lou. *Crikey.*

I went home that afternoon and sat by myself, doing puzzle after puzzle. I thought about Lightning Lou and Lucy. But mostly about Stringbean Noonan. Just a skinny kid who nobody noticed much. He wanted to be friends with a TV star.

Go figure.

I picked up the last puzzle piece. I turned it this way and that way in my hand. Then I

slid it into place. Suddenly, Rags—our living, drooling doorbell—started barking. My clock read exactly 3:59. Stringbean Noonan, I figured. Right on time.

"Here's the money I owe you," Stringbean said.

I took the money and nodded.

Stringbean sighed a little sadly, then turned to leave.

"Hey, Stringbean," I called out. "Catch."

Lightning Lou's hat sailed through the air and into his hands.

Stringbean's eyes widened. Without thinking, he put it on his head. Stringbean smiled brightly beneath the brim.

"It looks good on you," I said. "Keep it."

"What?! Keep it? Really?" he stammered.

"Sure," I replied. "Besides, I prefer my old hat."

"Thanks, Jigsaw," Stringbean said. "Thanks a lot."

He took a step toward me. Then another. At first, I was afraid he wanted to hug me. But instead, he sneezed.

Ah-choo!

"Bless you," I said. Then I went inside to change my shirt. Yuck!

Read on for a special sneak peek at
a brand-new, never-before-published
JIGSAW JONES MYSTERY:

The Case of the
Hat Burglar

"Highly recommended."—*School Library Journal*
on *Jigsaw Jones: The Case from Outer Space*

It's their toughest case yet . . . Will this be the first
mystery Jigsaw Jones and Mila *can't* solve?

Our Toughest Case

It reads "Theodore Jones" on my birth certificate. But, please, do me a favor. Don't call me that. My real name is Jigsaw.

Jigsaw Jones.

The way I see it, people should be able to make up their own names. After all, we're the ones who are stuck with them all our lives. Right? I get it. Our parents had to call us something when we were little—like "Biff" or "Rocko" or "Hey You!" But by age six, we should be allowed to name ourselves.

So I did. I took Jigsaw and tossed "Theodore" into the dumpster. These days, only two people call me Theodore. My mother, when she's unhappy. And my classmate Bobby Solofsky, when he wants to be annoying. Which is pretty much all the time. Bobby is a pain in my neck. Let me put it this way. Have you ever stepped on a Lego with your bare feet? There you are, cozy and sleepy, shuffling down the hallway in your pajamas, when suddenly—YOWZA!—you feel a stabbing pain in your foot.

What happened?

The Lego happened, that's what.

In my world, that Lego is named Bobby Solofsky.

And I'm the foot that stepped on it.

So, please, call me Jigsaw. After all, it's the name on the card.

NEED A MYSTERY SOLVED?

Call **Jigsaw Jones**
or **Mila Yeh**,
Private Eyes!

Mila is my partner and my best friend on the planet. I trust her 100 percent. Together, we make a pretty good team. We solve mysteries: lost bicycles, creepy scarecrows, surprise visitors from outer space, you name it. Put a dollar in our pockets, and we'll solve the case. Sometimes we do it for free.

But the Hat Burglar had us stumped.

We were baffled, bewildered, and bamboozled. There was a thief in our school, and I couldn't catch him. Or her. Because you never know about thieves. It could be anybody—he, she, or even it. That's true. *It happens.* We once caught a ferret red-handed. Or red-footed. Or red-pawed. Whatever! Point is, the ferret did it. But in this case, no matter what Mila and I tried, nothing worked. The mystery stayed a mystery. It was our toughest case yet. And by the end, the solution very nearly broke my heart.

But let me back up a bit. It all began last week, on a frosty Tuesday afternoon . . .

Frozen

It was the coldest day of the year. Three degrees below zero. In other words, it felt like the planet Hoth from *Star Wars*. Or Canada, maybe. Even worse, there wasn't a single snowflake on the ground. Just cold wind and frozen skies. It was so nasty my dog, Rags, didn't want to go outside. And Rags *lives* for going outside. That morning, he stood by the open door, cold wind blasting his nose, and whined. "Sorry, Rags," my father insisted. "I don't like it any more than you do. But we gotta go."

Rags put on the brakes.

Eventually, my father talked Rags into it. I think he promised a treat. Looking outside, I felt the same way. I didn't want to leave my toasty house, either. But when my mother said, "Time for the bus, Jigsaw, no dillydallying," I had no choice.

My mother lets me dilly. And she lets me dally. But I can never dillydally. That's going too far. Not when there's a bus to catch.

At the bus stop, several kids stood together like a bunch of Popsicles in a freezer. I knew that two of them were Mila and Joey Pignattano, but it was hard to tell who was

who. Almost everyone was bundled in thick winter clothes, hats pulled down to their eyeballs. "Murfle, murfle," somebody mumbled to me through a wool scarf. I murfled back.

The wind snarled as if it were a snaggletoothed wolf.

Once the bus dropped us at school, we headed for our classrooms. Geetha Nair walked into room 201, dressed in a long colorful scarf wrapped around (and around!) her neck and face. The only part of her head that showed through were two round, chocolate-brown eyes.

Helen Zuckerman burst through the door. "I can't feel my nose," she announced. "It's frozen solid. I could snap it off like an icicle."

Joey poked Helen's nose with a finger. "Yipes, you're right, Helen. It's colder than ice cream."

Bigs Maloney, in contrast, strolled in wearing shorts and a long-sleeve shirt. "No coat, Bigs?" Ms. Gleason asked.

"It's in my backpack," he explained. "Just in case."

"Bigs, it's below zero outside. When are you going to put on a pair of long pants?" Helen wondered.

The big lug shrugged. "I like shorts better. They let my knees breathe."

"I wish it would snow," curly haired Lucy Hiller muttered. "I don't mind the cold if there's snow. Then we could go sledding . . . or build snow forts . . . or—"

"Make snow pies!" Joey cried.

"What?" Mila swung her backpack around with one hand. It landed softly at the bottom of her cubby. "Seriously, Joey. Snow pies?"

"Yes," Joey replied. "Snow pies are delicious. Only one ingredient: fresh, white, delicious snow. Yum!"

Stringbean Noonan gasped and pointed at Mila's hands. "Look, it's so cold your fingers turned purple!"

Mila laughed. She wiggled her fingers. "It's only nail polish, Stringbean. I had them done at the mall with Geetha and my stepmom this weekend."

"Phew!" said Stringbean. He seemed relieved.

Athena Lorenzo staggered into the room. "My hair. It was wet when I left my house. Now it's frozen solid!"

"Oh, Athena. Don't you have a hat?" Ms. Gleason asked.

"I used to," Athena said. "I think I lost it in school yesterday."

"Well, that's a problem," Ms. Gleason said. "Hats keep heads warm. It's important protection in this weather. Athena, do you know where we keep our Lost and Found?"

Athena shrugged. "I guess I lost that, too."

Ms. Gleason looked at me. I gave her a nod to let her know that I knew. "Jigsaw, could you please accompany Athena to the Lost and Found?"

Thank you for reading this **FEIWEL AND FRIENDS** book.

The Friends who made

The Case of the
Bear Scare

possible are:

Jean Feiwel, Publisher

Liz Szabla, Associate Publisher

Rich Deas, Senior Creative Director

Holly West, Senior Editor

Anna Roberto, Senior Editor

Val Otarod, Associate Editor

Kat Brzozowski, Senior Editor

Alexei Esikoff, Senior Managing Editor

Raymond Ernesto Colón, Senior Production Manager

Anna Poon, Assistant Editor

Emily Settle, Assistant Editor

Erin Siu, Editorial Assistant

Patrick Collins, Creative Director

Taylor Pitts, Production Editor

Follow us on Facebook or visit us online at mackids.com.

OUR BOOKS ARE FRIENDS FOR LIFE.